Choose Some Shoes!

T0337813

Written by Mary Roulston
Illustrated by Alicia Arlandis

Collins

Who's in this story?

Listen and say

Download the audio at www.collins.co.uk/839770

Mum

Meltem

Ali

Meltem, Ali and Mum are at the shoe shop. They want new shoes.

Meltem sees some brown boots.
She puts on the boots.

5

Meltem says, "I can walk in these boots!"

Meltem takes off the brown boots.

She sees some blue sports shoes.
She puts on the sports shoes.

Meltem says, "I can play football now!"

Meltem says, "We are winning!"

Meltem takes off the blue shoes.

There are some green boots.
She puts on the boots.

Meltem says, "I can walk in the water in these boots."

Wow!
Look at the fish!

Meltem sees some white shoes.
They are beautiful. She puts on
the shoes.

Meltem says, "I can dance and jump in these shoes!"

I don't like those shoes!

19

Meltem doesn't like the shoes, but she loves school!

Meltem says, "I can do and learn lots of things in these shoes!"

Picture dictionary

Listen and repeat

boots

climb

put on

shoes

sports shoes

take off

win

1 Look and order the story

2 Listen and say

Collins

Published by Collins
An imprint of HarperCollins*Publishers*
Westerhill Road
Bishopbriggs
Glasgow
G64 2QT

HarperCollins*Publishers*
1st Floor, Watermarque Building
Ringsend Road
Dublin 4
Ireland

William Collins' dream of knowledge for all began with the publication of his first book in 1819.

A self-educated mill worker, he not only enriched millions of lives, but also founded a flourishing publishing house. Today, staying true to this spirit, Collins books are packed with inspiration, innovation and practical expertise. They place you at the centre of a world of possibility and give you exactly what you need to explore it.

© HarperCollins*Publishers* Limited 2020

10 9 8 7 6 5 4 3 2

ISBN 978-0-00-839770-8

Collins® and COBUILD® are registered trademarks of HarperCollins*Publishers* Limited

www.collins.co.uk/elt

British Library Cataloguing in Publication Data

A catalogue record for this publication is available from the British Library.

Author: Mary Roulston
Illustrator: Alicia Arlandis (Beehive)
Series editor: Rebecca Adlard
Commissioning editor: Fiona Undrill
Publishing manager: Lisa Todd
Product managers: Jennifer Hall and Caroline Green
In-house editor: Alma Puts Keren
Project manager: Emily Hooton
Editor: Tessie Papadopoulou-Dalton
Proofreaders: Natalie Murray and Michael Lamb
Cover designer: Kevin Robbins
Typesetter: 2Hoots Publishing Services Ltd
Audio produced by id audio, London
Reading guide author: Emma Wilkinson
Production controller: Rachel Weaver
Printed and bound by: GPS Group, Slovenia

Download the audio for this book and a reading guide for parents and teachers at www.collins.co.uk/839770